W9-BRC-470

THE MYSTERIOUS TADPOLE

To Helen,
with ever-growing gratitude
and love

The Mysterious Tadpole

NEW ILLUSTRATIONS AND TEXT BY

STEVEN KELLOGG

PUFFIN BOOKS

"Greetings, nephew!" cried Louis's uncle McAllister. "I've brought a wee bit of Scotland for your birthday."

"Thanks!" said Louis. "Look, Mom and Dad. It's a TADPOLE!"

Louis named him Alphonse and promised to take very good care of him.

Louis took Alphonse to school for show-and-tell.

"Class, here we have a splendid example of a tadpole," exclaimed Ms. Shelbert. "Let's ask Louis to bring it back every week so we can watch it become a frog."

Ms. Shelbert was amazed to see how quickly Alphonse grew. "Maybe it's because he only eats cheeseburgers," said Louis.

When Alphonse became too big for his jar, Louis moved him to the kitchen sink. "He's the perfect pet!" said Louis.

Louis and Alphonse loved to play games.

"Be careful, Louis," said his mother. "The living room is not a soccer field. Something is going to get broken!"

And she was right. That same day the soccer ball slammed into Aunt Tabitha's antique lamp.

"This tadpole is out of control," said Louis's mother. "Something must be done."

"It won't happen again," promised Louis. "I'll take Alphonse to obedience school."

The only animals at the obedience school were dogs. Some of their owners stared at Alphonse suspiciously.

"Pretend you're a dog," whispered Louis.

Alphonse tried to bark, but it sounded like a burp.

"Hold on a minute," said the trainer. "What kind of dog is this?"
"He's a hairless spotted water spaniel from Scotland," explained Louis.

Alphonse quickly learned to SIT, STAY, and RETRIEVE. He graduated at the top of his class.
"My parents will be very pleased," said Louis.

But Louis's parents were not pleased when Alphonse outgrew the sink and had to be moved to the bathtub.

"This shower is too crowded," complained Louis's father.
"This bathroom is a mess," moaned Louis's mother.

At least Louis's classmates enjoyed Alphonse, who was still making weekly visits.

"Wow! Show-and-tell is more fun than recess!" they yelled.

But one day Ms. Shelbert decided that Alphonse was not turning into an ordinary frog. She asked Louis to stop bringing him to school.

By the time summer vacation arrived, Alphonse had outgrown the bathtub.

"We could buy the parking lot next door and build him a swimming pool," suggested Louis.

"Be sensible," declared Louis's parents. "Swimming pools are expensive. We're sorry, Louis, but this situation has become impossible. Tomorrow you will have to take your tadpole to the zoo."

"But I can't put my friend in a cage!" cried Louis.

That night Louis was very sad—until he remembered that the gym in the nearby high school had a swimming pool.

Louis hid Alphonse under a carpet and smuggled him inside. "Nobody uses this place during the summer," whispered Louis. "You'll be safe here."

After making sure that Alphonse felt at home, Louis said good-bye. "I'll be back tomorrow with a big pile of cheeseburgers," he promised.

Louis came every afternoon to play with Alphonse. In the mornings he earned the money for the cheeseburgers by delivering newspapers.

The training continued as well.
Louis would say, "Alphonse, RETRIEVE!"

And Alphonse would succeed every time.

As summer vacation passed, Louis became more and more worried about what would happen to Alphonse when the high school kids returned.

After his first day of classes Louis ran to the high school, and found the gym bustling with activity. The swim team was heading for the pool.

"STOP!" cried Louis.

"On your mark!" bellowed the coach. "Get set!"
"Excuse me, sir," said Louis.

"GO!" roared the coach.

Alphonse rose to the surface to welcome the swimmers.

"It's a submarine from another planet!" shrieked the coach.
"Call the police! Call the Navy!"

"No, it's only a tadpole," said Louis. "He's my pet."

The coach was upset and confused.

"You have until tomorrow," he cried, "to get that creature out of the pool!"

Louis telephoned his friend Ms. Seevers, the librarian, and asked for her help.

"I'll be right there!" she said.

Ms. Seevers rushed to meet Louis at the high school. When she saw Alphonse, she was so startled that she dropped her purse into the water.

"RETRIEVE!" said Louis. And Alphonse did.

"Where did this astounding animal come from?" cried Ms. Seevers.

"He was a birthday gift from my uncle," Louis replied.

Ms. Seevers telephoned Uncle McAllister.

"Oh, the wee tadpole?" he said. "Why, he came from the lake nearby. It's the one folks call Loch Ness."

"Brace yourself, Louis!" Ms. Seevers said. "I believe your uncle found the Loch Ness monster!"

"I don't care!" cried Louis. "Alphonse is my friend and I love him." He pleaded with Ms. Seevers to help him raise enough money to buy the parking lot so he could build a big swimming pool for Alphonse.

Suddenly Ms. Seevers had an idea. "Long ago a pirate ship sank in the harbor," she said. "No one has ever been able to find it—or its treasure chest. But perhaps we can!"

The next morning they drove to the harbor and rented a boat. "This is a treasure chest," cried Louis. "RETRIEVE!"

Alphonse disappeared under the water . . .

. . . and returned with the chest! It was filled with gold and jewels. "Let's buy the parking lot and get to work!" cried Ms. Seevers.

Louis's parents were shocked to see a construction crew in the parking lot.

"Louis!" they cried. "What in the world is going on here?"

"Alphonse found a pirate treasure ship," explained Louis. "And we used part of our gold to buy you this present."

Louis's parents were shocked once again. "Tickets for a vacation cruise to Hawaii!" they gasped.

"And," said Louis, "you don't have to worry about us, because Granny has agreed to baby-sit."

They hugged Louis. They kissed Alphonse.

"How soon can we leave?" they cried.

"Immediately," said Louis.

By the time Louis's parents returned, the swimming pool was being enjoyed by everyone in the city.

A week later Louis said, "Alphonse, tomorrow is my birthday, which means that you've been my best friend for a whole year."

The next day Uncle McAllister arrived for the party.
"Greetings, Louis my lad!" he exclaimed. "I've come with a curious stone from the hills of Scotland. Happy birthday!"

"Wow! Thanks!" said Louis.
Suddenly the stone began to tremble and crack . . .

A Note from the Author

It is hard for me to believe that Alphonse and his loyal friend Louis have celebrated twenty-five birthdays since *The Mysterious Tadpole* was first published. When the editors suggested that I consider putting together a revised and re-illustrated anniversary edition, I eagerly accepted the invitation. With the passing years I realized there were nuances of character, sequence, and plot that I wished I had explored in the original version, and now I had the chance! I was particularly happy to create new pictures that would not be confined by the limitations of pre-separation (the illustration technique that the economics of printing had demanded the first time). It was enormously satisfying to approach the images with the heightened control, expressivity, and enjoyment that full-color printing makes possible. Now Louis, Alphonse, and their friends can be seen exactly as I saw them in my mind's eye all those years ago.

PUFFIN BOOKS
Published by Penguin Group
Penguin Young Readers Group,
345 Hudson Street, New York, New York 10014, U.S.A.
Penguin Books Ltd, 80 Strand, London WC2R ORL, England
Penguin Books Canada Ltd, 10 Alcorn Avenue, Toronto, Ontario, Canada M4V 3B2

First published in the United States of America by Dial Books for Young Readers,
a division of Penguin Putnam Inc., 2002
Published by Puffin Books, a division of Penguin Young Readers Group, 2004

1 3 5 7 9 10 8 6 4 2

Copyright © 2002 by Steven Kellogg
All rights reserved

Designed by Lily Malcom
The full-color artwork was prepared using ink and pencil line, watercolor washes, and acrylic paints.
The text of this book is set in Trump Mediaeval.

THE LIBRARY OF CONGRESS HAS CATALOGED THE DIAL EDITION AS FOLLOWS:
Kellogg, Steven.
The mysterious tadpole / Steven Kellogg. p. cm.
"25th Anniversary edition."
Summary: It soon becomes clear that Louis's pet tadpole is not turning into an ordinary frog.
ISBN: 0-8037-2788-7
[1. Pets—Fiction.] I. Title. PZ7.K292 Mw 2002 [E]—dc21 2001053776

Puffin Books ISBN 0-14-240140-4

Manufactured in China

Except in the United States of America, this book is sold subject to the condition that it shall not,
by way of trade or otherwise, be lent, re-sold, hired out, or otherwise circulated without the publisher's
prior consent in any form of binding or cover other than that in which it is published and without
a similar condition including this condition being imposed on the subsequent purchaser.